The Chick
and the Duckling

Translated from the Russian of V. Suteyev

by Mirra Ginsburg
Pictures by Jose Aruego & Ariane Dewey

Macmillan/McGraw-Hill School Publishing Company

New York   Chicago   Columbus

For information regarding permission, write to Macmillan Publishing Company,
866 Third Avenue, New York, NY 10022.

This edition is reprinted by arrangement with Macmillan Publishing Company,
a division of Macmillan, Inc.

The text was translated from the Russian *Tsyplenok i Utenok*
(The Chick and the Duckling) of V. Suteyev.

The four-color illustrations were prepared as pen-and-ink line drawings with
halftone overlays. The typeface is Avant Garde Book.
1995 Printing
Macmillan/McGraw-Hill School Division
10 Union Square East
New York, New York 10003

Printed in the United States of America

ISBN 0-02-179091-4 / 1, L. 1

5 6 7 8 9   FED   99 98 97 96 95 94

to Libby

⬭   ⬭

A Duckling came out
of the shell.

"I am out!" he said.

"Me too," said the Chick.

"I am taking a walk,"
said the Duckling.

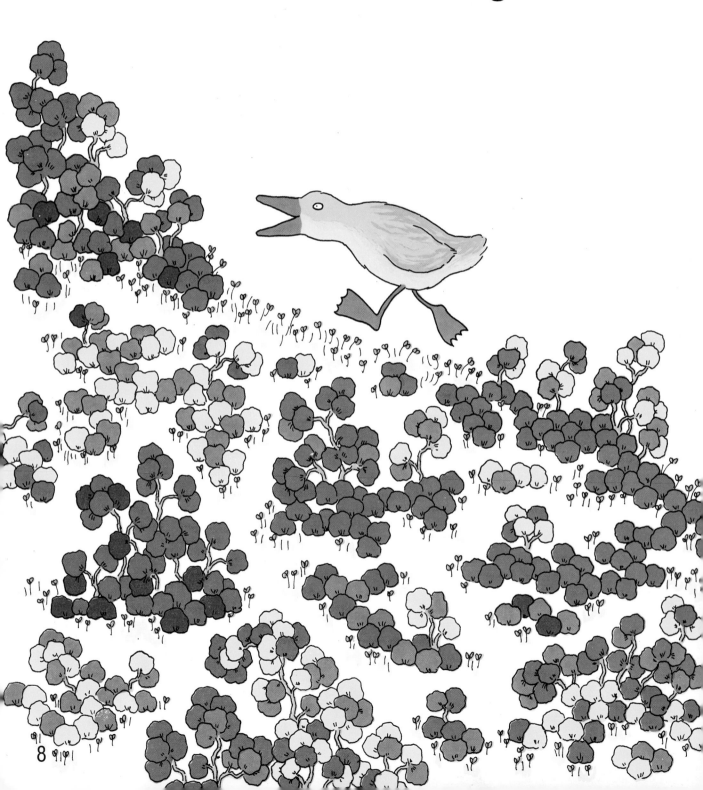

"Me too,"
said the Chick.

"I am digging a hole,"
said the Duckling.

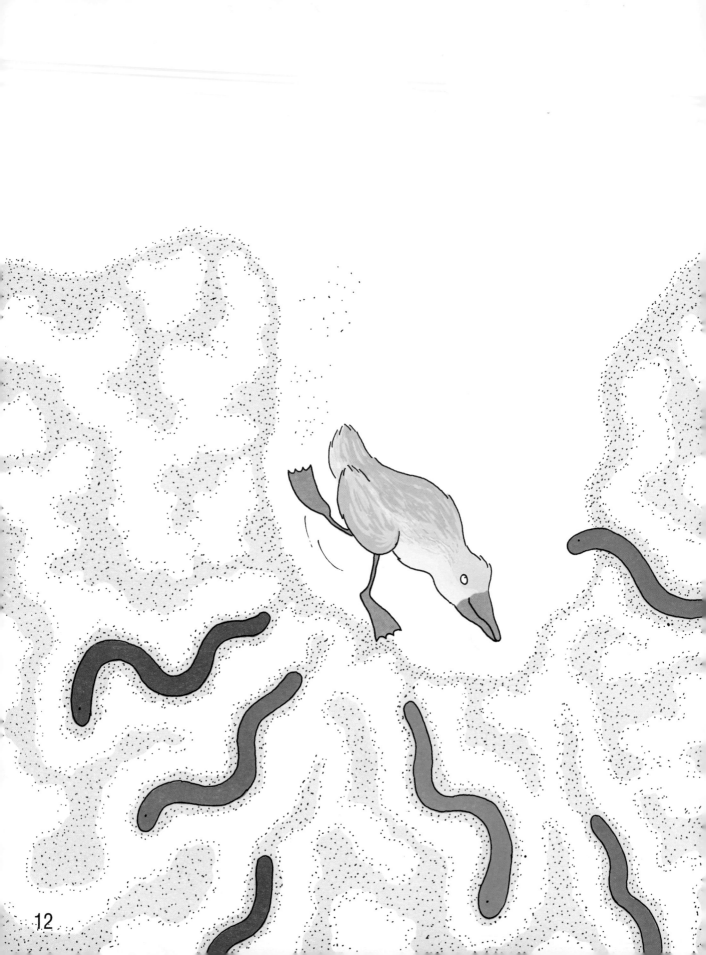

"Me too,"
said the Chick.

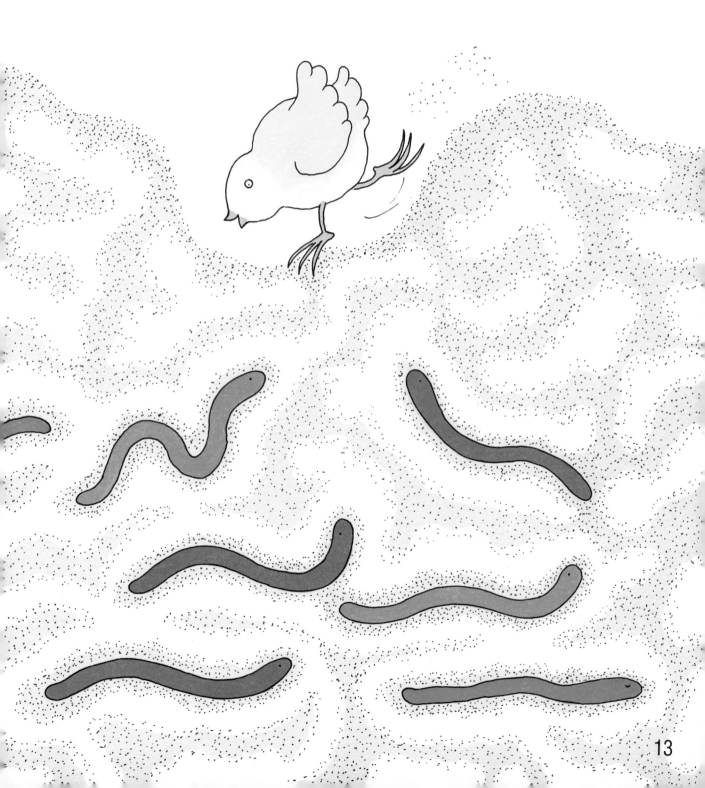

"I found a worm,"
said the Duckling.

"Me too,"
said the Chick.

"I caught
a butterfly,"
said the
Duckling.

"Me too,"
said the Chick.

"I am going for a swim,"
said the Duckling.

"Me too,"
said the Chick.

"I am swimming,"
said the Duckling.

"Me too!"
cried the Chick.

The Duckling pulled
the Chick out.

"I'm going for another swim," said the Duckling.

"Not me,"
said the Chick.

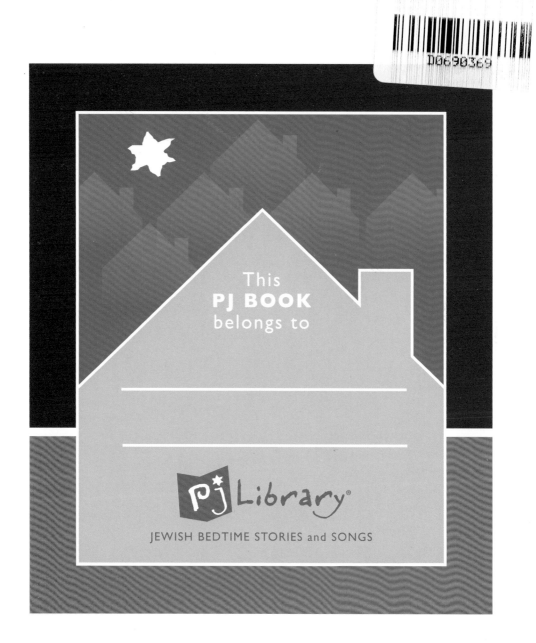

This
PJ BOOK
belongs to

_____

_____

PJ Library®

JEWISH BEDTIME STORIES and SONGS

PJ Library, a program of The Harold Grinspoon Foundation
67 Hunt Street, Suite 100
Agawam, MA 01001
U.S.A.

www.pjlibrary.org

First Edition
10 9 8 7 6 5 4 3 2 1
101421.2K1

Fridays Are Special

written by Chris Barash

illustrated by Melissa Iwai

I snuggled in my bed last night;
soft Moon looked down on me.

Now peeking from the covers,
bright Sun is what I see.

My daddy's in the kitchen.
His hair and hands are white.
I smell the Friday challah –
we'll all eat some tonight.

FLOUR

OIL

Cold air tingles on my cheeks;
soft mittens warm my hands.
Tovah's tugging on my scarf.
Snow sparkles as it lands.

Mommy lifts me way up high.
I help pick leafy greens.
Friday nights are special:
we eat like kings and queens!

LETTUCE

Nana holds me on her lap
for stories and a song.
Tovah cuddles up with us;
she likes to sing along.

Who's that knocking at the door?
My cousins Ben and Jake!

Yum! I smell warm cinnamon
from Nana's apple cake.

The sun is almost gone now.
My family gathers 'round.
Coins *plink*
plank in Grandpa's vest.
It's his tzedakah sound.

We all stand by the mantle.
The candles shine so bright.
I peek between my fingers.
It's such a pretty sight.

The matzah balls are fluffy and the challah tastes so sweet. I crawl under the table – so many legs and feet!

My favorite blanket hugs me;
a pillow holds my head.
Sh'ma is whispered like a breath.
I cuddle in my bed.

High in the sky, stars twinkle.
I close my sleepy eyes –
safe and warm until I wake
to see Shabbat's Sun rise.